CUDDLE ME HAPPY
A Collection of Stories for Sharing

LITTLE TIGER PRESS
An imprint of Magi Publications
1 The Coda Centre, 189 Munster Road,
London SW6 6AW
www.littletigerpress.com

First published in Great Britain 2010
This volume copyright
© Magi Publications 2010
Cover illustration copyright
© Caroline Pedler 2007

DORA'S EGGS
Julie Sykes
Illustrated by Jane Chapman
First published in Great Britain 1997
by Little Tiger Press,
an imprint of Magi Publications
Text copyright © Julie Sykes 1997
Illustrations copyright © Jane Chapman 1997

HAPPY BIRTHDAY, DOTTY!
Tim Warnes
First published in Great Britain 2003
by Little Tiger Press,
an imprint of Magi Publications
Text and illustrations copyright
© Tim Warnes 2003

HUNGRY HARRY
Joanne Partis
First published in Great Britain 2000
by Little Tiger Press,
an imprint of Magi Publications
Text and illustrations copyright
© Joanne Partis 2000

BIG BEARS CAN!
David Bedford
Illustrated by Gaby Hansen
First published in Great Britain 2001
by Little Tiger Press,
an imprint of Magi Publications
Text copyright © David Bedford 2001
Illustrations copyright © Gaby Hansen 2001

Cuddle me Happy

A Collection of Stories for Sharing

LITTLE TIGER PRESS

Contents

DORA'S EGGS

by Julie Sykes

illustrated by Jane Chapman

Dora was sitting on a nest of eggs.
They were shiny brown and smooth
to touch.

"These are my very first eggs,"
clucked Dora proudly. "I must
get all my friends to come and
admire them."

Dora climbed out of the henhouse
and into the farmyard.
  "Who shall I visit first?" she wondered.
"I know! I'll go and find Debbie Duck."

Dora hopped over the fence and across
the field until she reached the pond.

"Hello, Debbie," she called. "Would you
like to come and see my eggs?"

"I can't come now," quacked Debbie.
"I'm teaching my babies to swim."

Dora stood watching the ducklings splashing around and learning to paddle. Somehow she felt a bit less excited.

"My eggs are nice," she thought. "But those fluffy ducklings are much nicer."

13

Dora was just a little sad as she trotted over to the sty to visit Penny Pig.

"Hello, Penny," she clucked. "Would you like to come and see my eggs?"

But Penny didn't hear. She was having too much fun tumbling around with her wriggly piglets.

Dora gave a little sigh.

"My eggs are nice," she said. "But those wriggly piglets are much nicer."

Dora gave another little sigh as she climbed
the hill to find Sally Sheep.

"Would you like to come and see my eggs?"
she asked Sally.

"Not today," bleated Sally. "I'm too busy
keeping an eye on my lambs."

Dora looked at the lambs
frolicking in the field.
She felt rather glum.
"My eggs are nice," she
thought. "But those playful
lambs are much nicer."

17

Very sadly, Dora walked back to the farmyard.
On her way she bumped into Daisy Dog.
  "Hello, Daisy," clucked Dora. "Would you like
to come and see my eggs?"
  "Sorry, Dora," barked Daisy, wagging her tail.
"I can't come now. I'm taking my puppies
for a walk."

Dora was beginning to feel
quite miserable.

"My eggs are nice," she thought.
"But those cute puppies out
for a walk are much nicer."

19

In the farmyard Dora stopped at the cow shed. She wished she felt happier—perhaps Clarissa the Cow would cheer her up.

"Would you like to see my eggs?" she called.

"Sssh," mooed Clarissa softly, nodding at the straw. Snuggled up by her feet was a newborn calf, fast asleep.

Dora wanted to cry.

"My eggs are nice," she whispered. "But that little calf all snuggled up is much nicer."

21

Dora walked back across the yard in the
sunlight and climbed into the henhouse.
Her eggs were just as she had left them,
smooth and brown and very still.

"My eggs are nice," sighed Dora, fluffing
out her feathers. "But everyone else's
babies are *much* nicer."

Very sadly, Dora settled
herself down onto
her nest . . .

CRACK!

Dora jumped up in surprise.

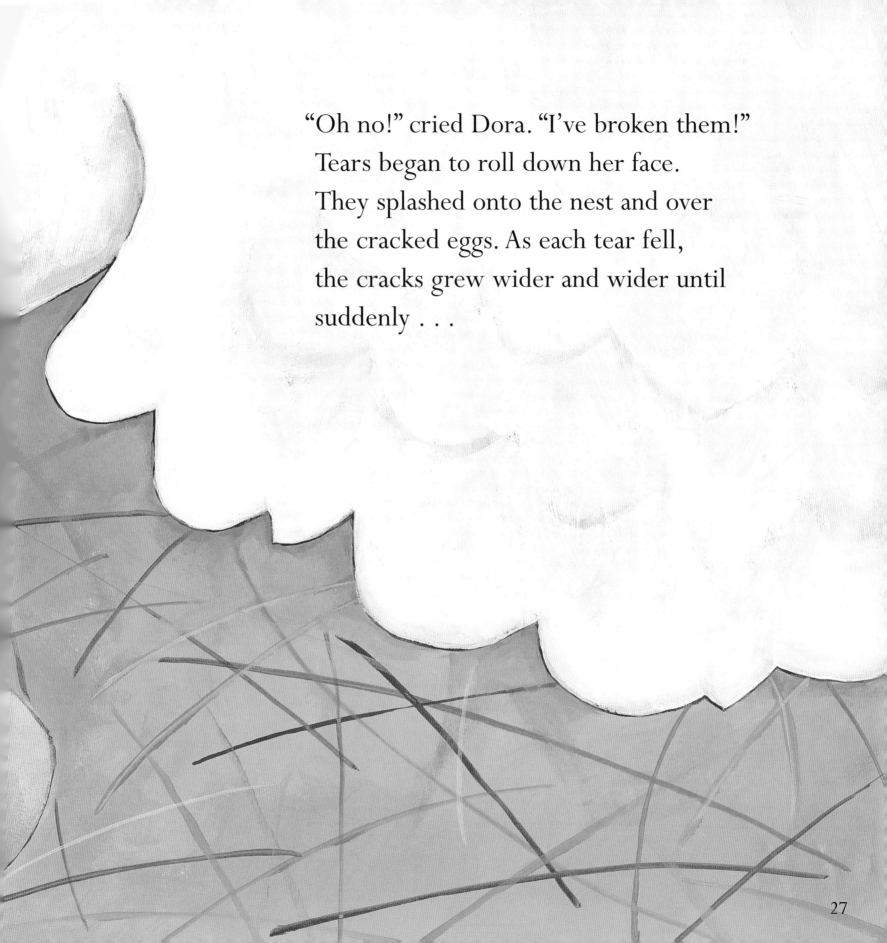

"Oh no!" cried Dora. "I've broken them!"
Tears began to roll down her face.
They splashed onto the nest and over
the cracked eggs. As each tear fell,
the cracks grew wider and wider until
suddenly . . .

. . . up popped a fluffy head,
then another, and another.

Soon the nest was full of
tiny chicks.

"Cheep, cheep," the chicks
peeped. "Cheep, cheep."
Dora stopped crying and
stared at her babies.

29

30

It didn't matter that the eggs were broken.
The new chicks were everything Dora had
ever wanted!

Proudly she strutted out into the farmyard,
and one by one the chicks followed after her.
All the animals stopped and looked.

"Why, Dora!" quacked Debbie.
"They're as fluffy as my ducklings!"
  "And wriggly like my piglets,"
oinked Penny.
  "They're as playful as my lambs,"
baaed Sally.
  "And you can take them for walks—
just like my puppies," barked Daisy.
  "But best of all," mooed Clarissa,
"your chicks can snuggle up to you,
like my calf snuggles up to me."
  "Cluck," said Dora happily, agreeing
with her friends. "My eggs were
nice, but my chicks are much,
much nicer!"

Tim Warnes

Happy Birthday, Dotty!

Dotty was very excited.

It was her birthday.

She had lots of cards
to open. But where were
all of Dotty's friends?

Dotty went to find Pip the mouse.
Instead she found a little round
present with her name on it!

What could it be?

Happy Birthday
Dotty!
Love from
Pip the mouse x

Hooray!

A bouncy ball!

As she chased after it for a bit, Dotty spotted an arrow on the floor. It pointed to another and another.

It was a birthday trail!
Dotty followed the arrows . . .

to the sandbox, where there was
another present. Dotty read the tag:
"Happy Birthday, Dotty! Love Tommy
the Tortoise."

What was it?

Delicious!

A yummy bone!

Dotty hurried across
the garden, following
the arrows to . . .

Susie's apple tree.
Leaning against
her nest was
another present!

49

Yippee!

It was a kite from Susie!

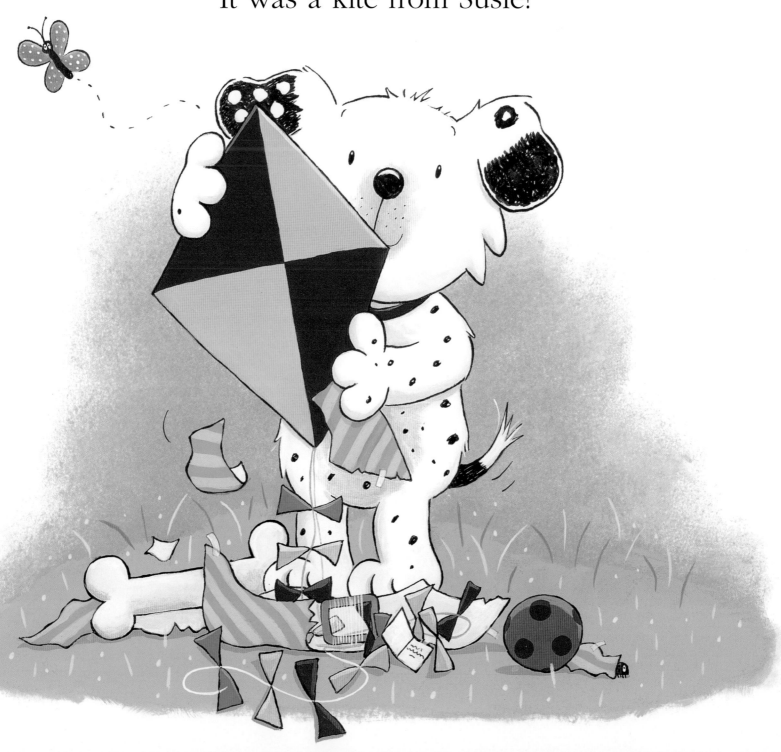

But Susie wasn't there to help fly it.
Where was everyone?

Dotty was puzzled.
Taking all her presents,
she skipped along the trail
of arrows to . . .

Whiskers the rabbit's hutch.

Dotty saw another funny-shaped present.

She read, "Happy Birthday, Dotty!

Love, Whiskers."

It was . . .

Wow!

A tricycle!

Dotty squealed with delight. She put all her presents into the tricycle's basket. She'd had lots of surprises, but Dotty's friends were still nowhere to be found.

Where could they be? Maybe they had followed the arrows too. Dotty climbed onto her shiny new tricycle and . . .

WHEEE!

She went to look for her friends.

56

Suddenly the trail ended.
Dotty was amazed to find . . .

. . . the
biggest present
she had ever seen!

Dotty danced around
and around in circles.
What could this be?

"Surprise!
Happy Birthday, Dotty!"

61

Joanne Partis

Hungry Harry

Harry Frog was feeling hungry.
"What's for dinner?" he asked his mom.
"Well, I think you're old enough to look for
your own food now," said Mommy Frog.

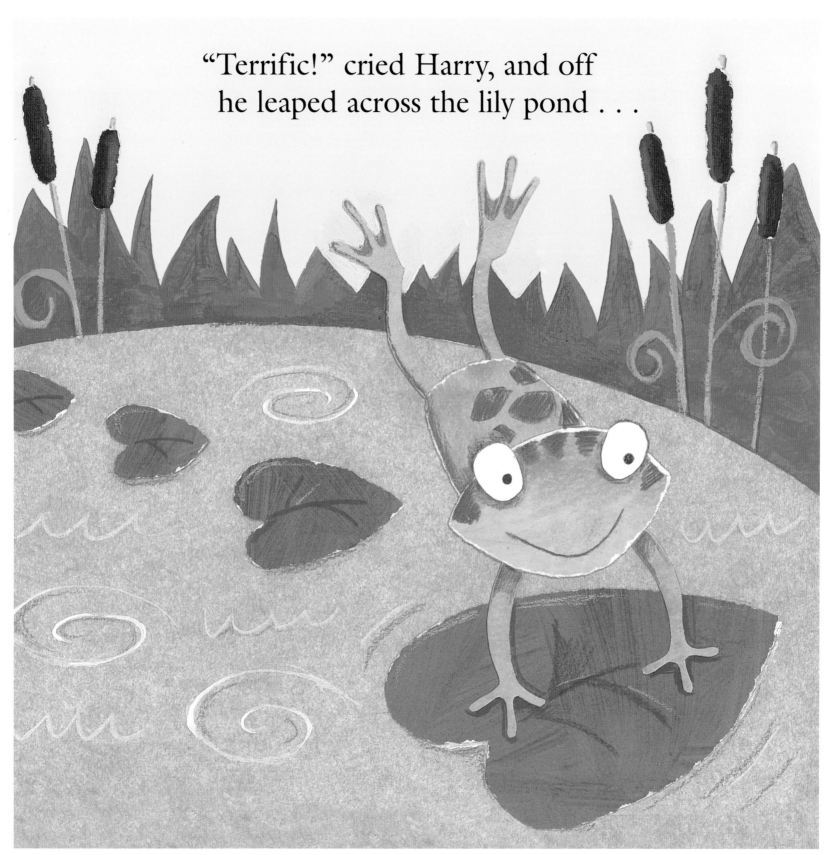

"Terrific!" cried Harry, and off
he leaped across the lily pond . . .

till he came to some tall reeds.
"There's sure to be something tasty
here," said Harry, licking his lips.

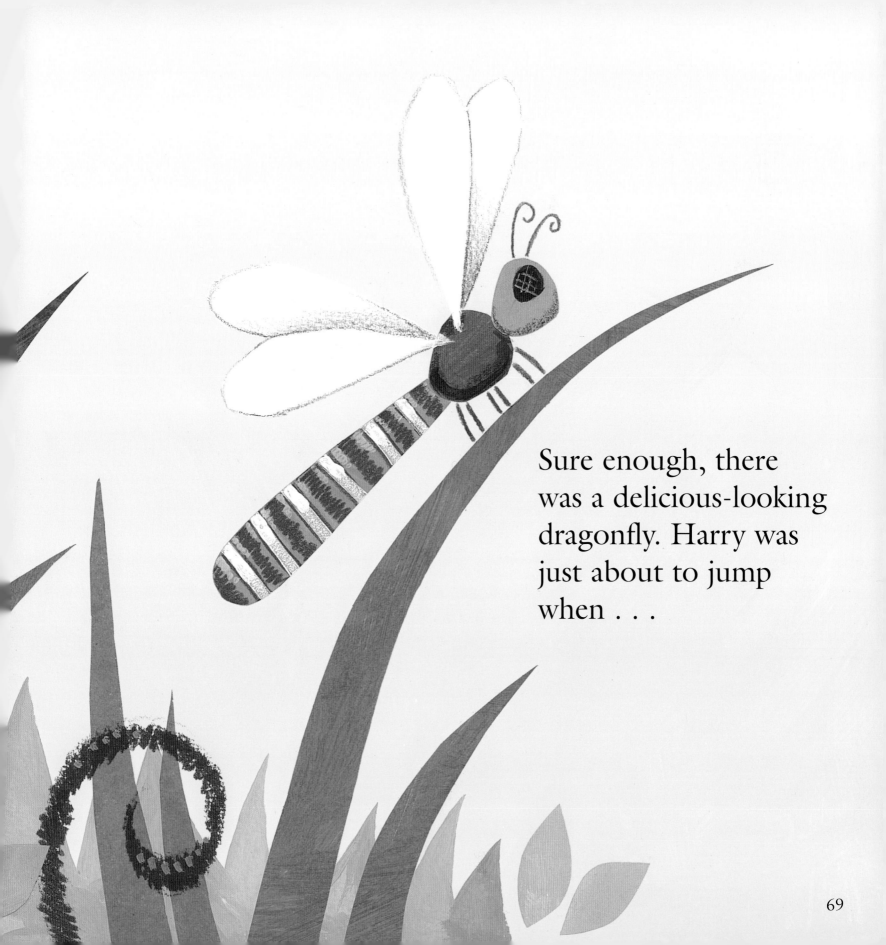

Sure enough, there
was a delicious-looking
dragonfly. Harry was
just about to jump
when . . .

69

the dragonfly flew off, high
into the air.
"You can't eat me!" she called.
"I'm much too quick for you."

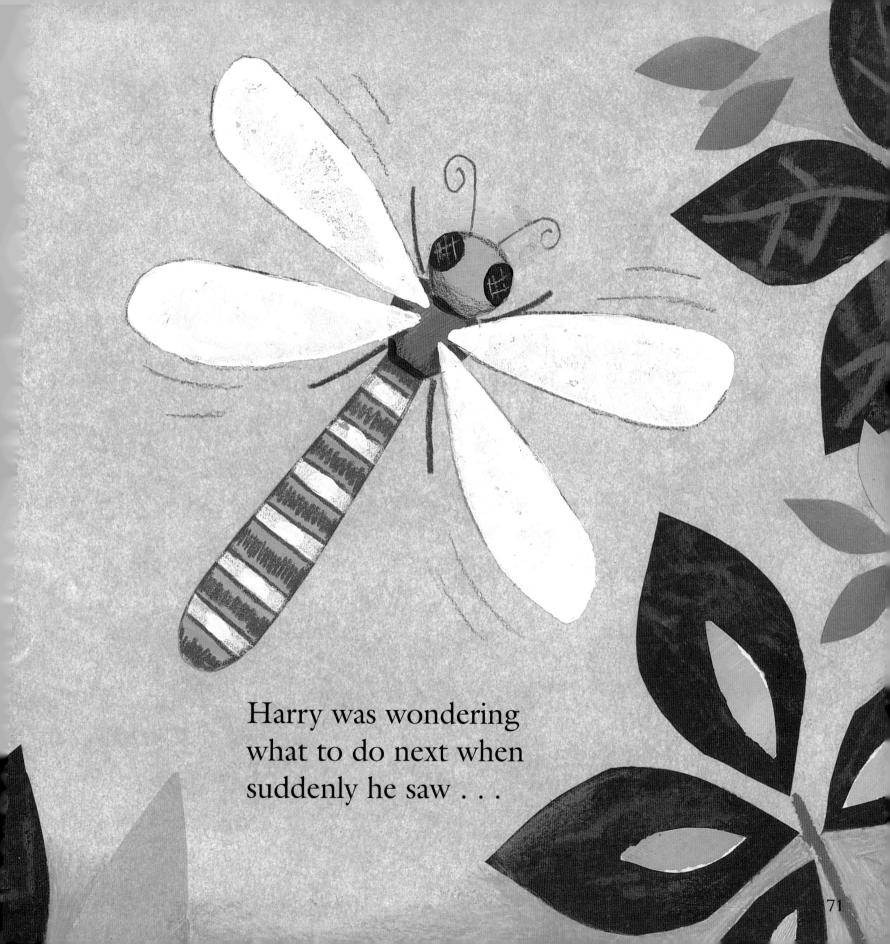

Harry was wondering
what to do next when
suddenly he saw . . .

a big juicy caterpillar
on a twig above him.

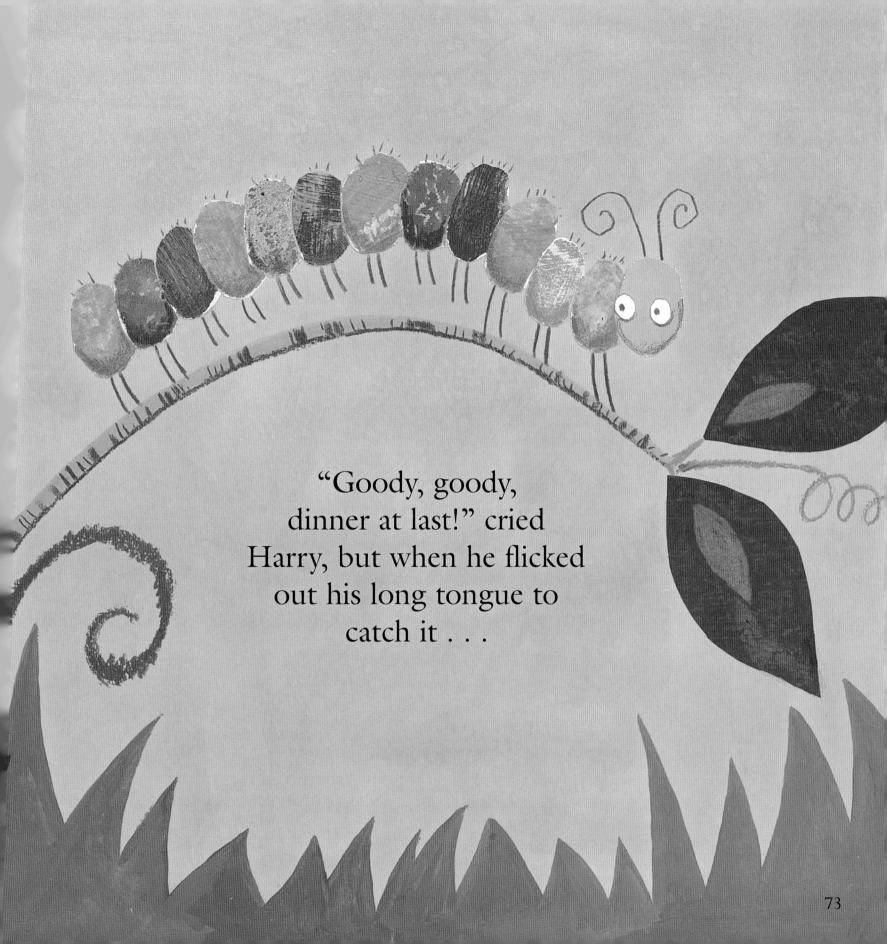

"Goody, goody,
dinner at last!" cried
Harry, but when he flicked
out his long tongue to
catch it . . .

the caterpillar
laughed.
"You can't eat me!"
she said.
"My hairs would
tickle your tongue."

74

"Never mind, I'll find something soon," said Harry.
He bounced on until he met . . .

a scrumptious-looking snail crawling towards him.

"Yummy, yummy," said Harry, but when he reached it . . .

the snail's head suddenly disappeared!
"You can't eat me!" said the
snail from inside its shell.
"I'm much too clever."

Harry was getting hungrier and hungrier.
He was just about to give up and go
home to his mom, when he spotted . . .

80

a squirmy worm,
wriggling along.
"Now's my chance!" cried
Harry, but just as he was
about to catch the worm
in his big wide mouth . . .

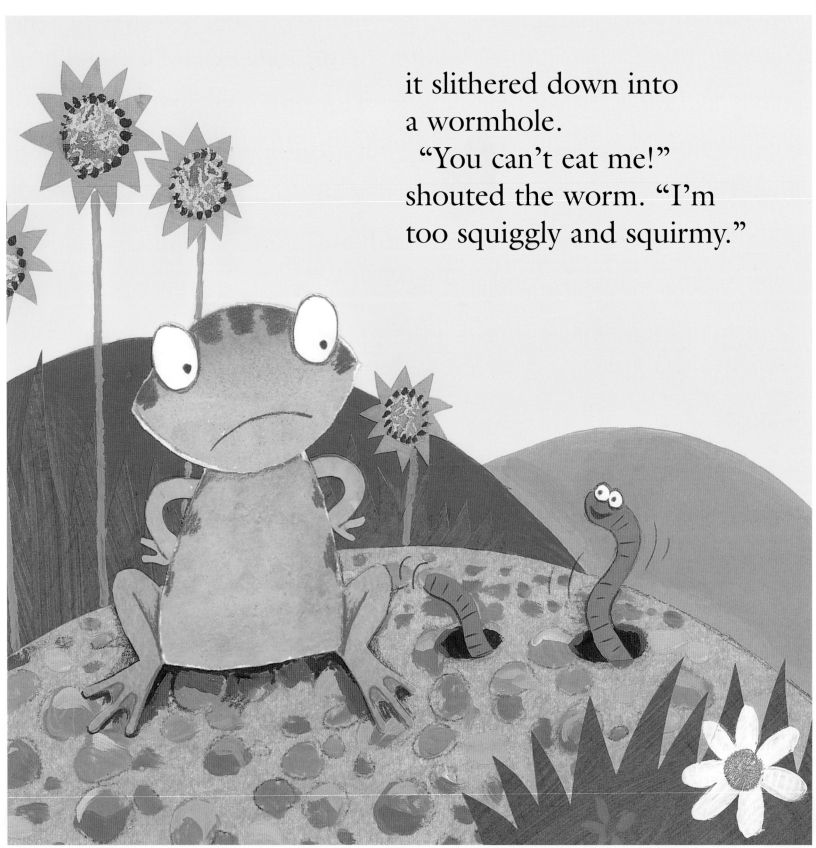

it slithered down into
a wormhole.
 "You can't eat me!"
shouted the worm. "I'm
too squiggly and squirmy."

Harry felt
very fed up. He
would go home to
his mom. But just
as he turned to
hop back, he saw
something he'd
never seen
before . . .

It didn't look too quick . . .

It didn't look too tickly . . .

It didn't look too clever . . .

And it didn't look
too squiggly and
squirmy.

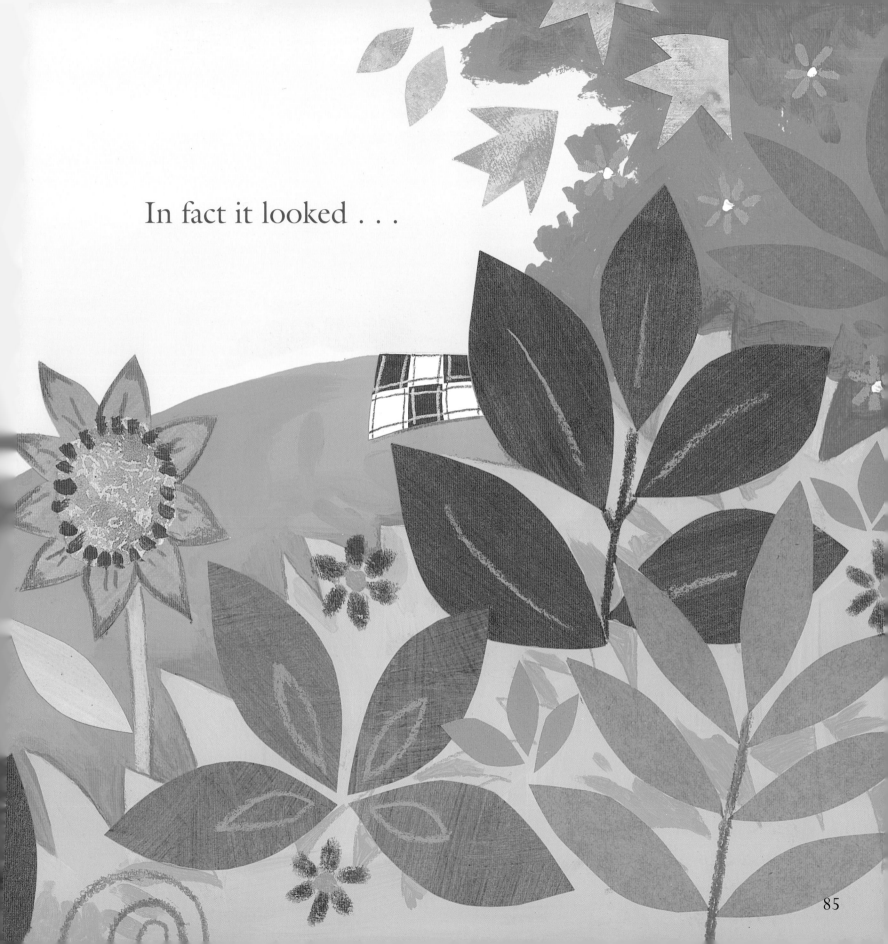

In fact it looked . . .

85

absolutely delicious!

And, what was more . . .

there was

88

enough for everyone!

David Bedford *and* Gaby Hansen

Big Bears Can!

Big Bear had to look after
Little Bear when Mommy
Bear went out.
  "Do I have to?" asked Big Bear.
  "Yes," said Mommy Bear.
"Just keep the house neat.
I won't be long."

95

"What can Big Bears do?" asked Little Bear
when Mommy Bear had gone.
  "Big Bears can do *everything*," said Big Bear.
  "Can they stand on their heads?"
  "Yes they can," said Big Bear.

"See!"

"But they can't do *this*," said Little Bear . . .

BOING! BOING!

"Of course they can,"
said Big Bear. "That's easy."

BOING!

"Oops!"

"Can you fix the springs?"
asked Little Bear.
"Yes," said Big Bear.
"I can."

"But you can't do *this*,"
said Little Bear. "No way."

"Big Bears don't swing," said
Big Bear. "That would be silly."
  "You're too big to swing,
anyway," said Little
Bear.

"NO I'M NOT," roared Big Bear. "Watch this!"

"Look out!"
said Little Bear.
"You're too heavy!"

"You've squashed Mommy's flowers, too," said Little Bear. "Can you fix everything?"
"I *hope* I can," said Big Bear.

"But you can't make
tunnels like this,"
said Little Bear.

"I don't want to make tunnels," said Big Bear. "I'm going to sit quietly until Mommy comes back."

"Big Bears *can't* do everything," sang Little Bear. "Big Bears *can't*, Big Bears *can't*, Big Bears CAN'T do everything." "YES THEY CAN!" said Big Bear.

"This is fun, isn't it!" said Big Bear.
"HERE COMES MOMMY," shouted
Little Bear. "She's going to be very angry."

"Big Bears can't hide," said
Little Bear.

"Yes they can," said Big Bear.
"Move over so I can squeeze
in beside you."

"There's not enough room,"
said Little Bear. "Mommy
will see you."

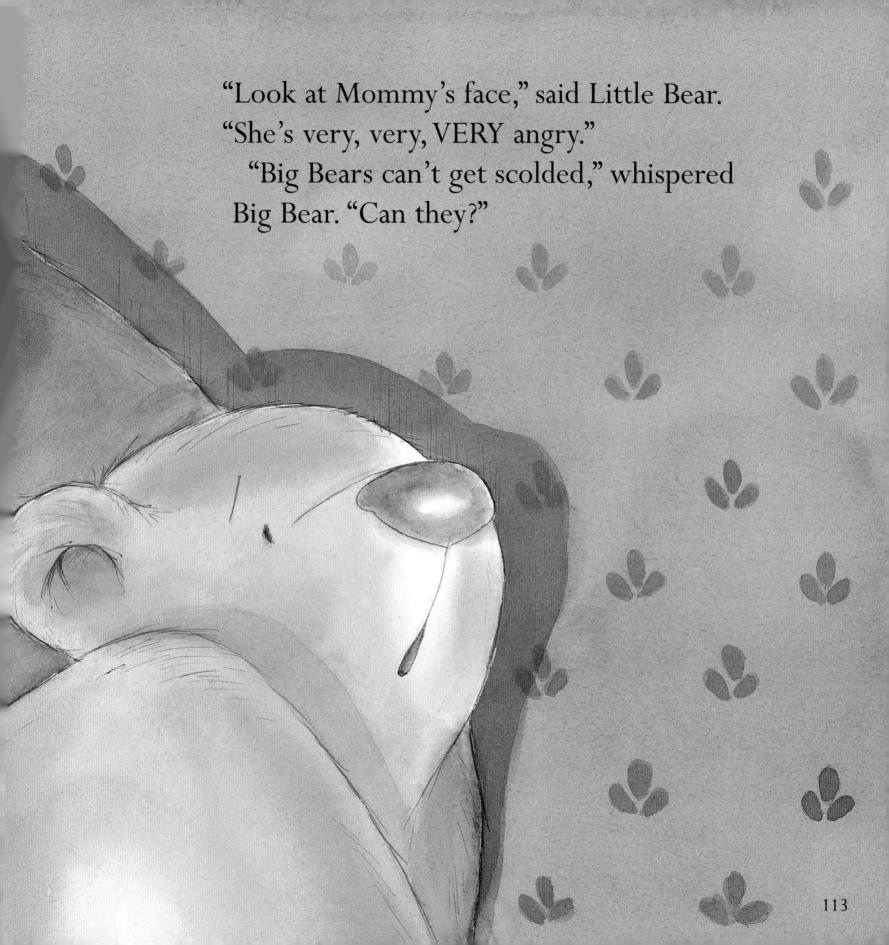

"Look at Mommy's face," said Little Bear. "She's very, very, VERY angry."

"Big Bears can't get scolded," whispered Big Bear. "Can they?"

113

YES THEY CAN!

Poor Big Bear. If only Little Bear
could make him feel better.

"Can Big Bears have hugs?" asked
Little Bear.

115

"Yes," said Big Bear.

"Big Bears can!"